Code 1000

Written By: Madison Ebejer

On a cold day in Fishten, west Virginia, Christian steed woke up to the ringing of her alarm clock it was 6:00 in the morning Christian got up slowly and yawned it was her first night stay in her new house. Christian had just moved from West Point Oregon and missed it more than anything in the world why did her dad make her move? She then walked down the cold tile floors to her own bathroom the new house was huge 3 stories high and had 12 bedrooms Christian hated the new house it was big and dark but she had to learn to deal with it. Christian started the water and locked the door because she new if she didn't her sister Zoe would walk in. Christian scrubbed herself clean got out and dried of when she got back in the bedroom it was only 7:30 time was going as slow as molasses. She walk into her huge walk in closet filled up barely with a quarter of cloths and picked out a part of teal all stars a orange shirt and some old ripped up jeans she heard a door slam from way down the hall Zoe was up and after only 45 minuets of peace Zoe came running through the door

"Hey big sister"

Zoe said in her annoying but cute 7 year-old voice hello Christian said blind of emotion and silently Zoe picked her hand up and dragged her down stairs. "Of course Christian thought to her self waffle breakfast as usual" it was a steed family tradition waffles every Sunday morning no matter what Christian didn't enjoy the waffle that her dad made without her mom the mornings were dry and awkward the only break of the silence was Zoe chiming in every so often with something that she thought would be fun to do that day but Christian knew that they hadn't done any special activity after her mom left. Christian didn't like to think of her mom to much it brought to much pain but with every attempt came nothing but these few words from her father

“She had a job that made it hard to have a family”

Christian new her dad wasn’t telling her everything but her dad seemed so timid and shy after she left that it was too hard to ask more.

Christian sat in one of the spots on the both table and looked outside the window everything was frosty and cold what couldn’t it be warm like in Oregon her dad then brought out plates butter and syrup and said

“Serve yourself”

In a trying to be cheerful way Christian thought “ha funny he cant notice that he just makes things awkward” but she could never say it she started chewing her dry pancakes and feeling sorry for her self.

Christian finished breakfast and hoped on her bike that had finally been delivered although she didn't know where many places were she new where the park was and swiftly rode there she parked her bike and walked to the swings where she sat down she noticed 3 blonde girls staring at her all with blue eyes and one had freckled and streaks of blue in her hair they looked at her and started laughing Christian wasn't beautiful with her mousy brown hair grey eyes pale skin and multiple freckles she new being new was hard but would people already dislike her . Christian didn't really care she looked around the park and saw 2 boys looking at her she could see them murmuring to them selves Christian thought this was really creepy and rode home. The only way Christian new witch house was hers was by the strange design of it with its stain glass windows and brick walls it was different from anyone's on the block for that matter in the whole town.

Aside from moving to a new house Christian had to go to a new school and she was not happy Christian had already been the new girl and she didn't enjoy it. Being new meant new friends and not to mention new enemies. Christian had never wanted to move but her dad said the house had to many bad memories her dad new she was angry at him for making the family move but he let her pick out the new house. Christian basically watched TV the rest of the day and went to bed at eight tomorrow was a big day her first day at her new school and she was avoiding it like the plague.

One: the first day

Christian woke up Monday February first it was her first day at her new school and she planed on being sick she walked out of bed to her closet mirror and brushed out her tangled hair she had purple circles around her eyes she hadn't had enough sleep she looked in her closet and picked out a white crop tee and but a blue shirt under it with a pair of old worn blue shorts she slipped on her teal converse got on her red back pack picked up a piece of toast and suddenly heard the buses horn it was time to go. Her sister grabbed her legs and she heard her dad yell

"I love you Christian"

He was already in his office. She walked out the front door to the bus and she walked up the steps slowly one at a time and when she got around the corner the 3 blonde girls seemed to be waiting the was a rush of whispers and laughter what was happening Christian thought why was the day already so miserable? She slinks silently to the back of the bus and sat down the bus seemed to be going 0 miles per hour when would this end the bus then rolled up to 2 houses and 2 boys walked out of the houses they where the 2 she saw from the park she new it was them because of how they look one had blonde hair down to his neck and blue eyes and very tan skin how was he so tan considering he lived here in just about the coldest place ever in Christians mind the other boy had curly brown hair brown eyes pale skin and lots of freckles ,after seeing them the first thought that came to her mind was more teasing but she was very wrong the 2 boys walked on the bus and the middle girl of the 3 said hey max to the boy with curly hair ummm hi Natasha max said dryly and walked to the back of the bus and sat down with Christian and the other boy sat down to

“Hi max said I’m max and this is my friend Costin”

“Um hi my names Christian, Christian steed”

And then they were quiet the rest of the ride to her new school the bus finally pulled in to the little yellow school that on a sign read in big letters honey bee middle school it had roses surrounding the perimeter of the front office and true to its name had lots of honey bees buzzing around.

Christian was stepping out of the bus she suddenly tripped Natasha started giggling and swiftly hopped down the steps. Christian got up and started to walk down the busy hall and found her 7th grade class room she hung up her red back pack and pulled out a book she walked down to the courtyard and started to read suddenly she felt someone sit down next to her it was max he said.

“Don’t let Natasha bother you she’s mean to everyone”

“Ummm thanks for the tip”

“Well we should get going or well be late for class follow me”

Christian followed max to class and found her self siting in a desk right next to Natasha her teacher Mr. Humphrey had introduced Christian to the class and had asked someone to show her around costing and max volunteered so it looked like shed be spending recess with them. Christian was the first to finish her math so she had time to finish her homework luckily there was only 30 minuets of math left until recess most kids took a long time to do math so there was no time to do spelling before recess it was time to take a one stop train to misery.

Christian got up and walked out of the class max and costing followed she turned around and said to them meaner than she meant to

"Are you just going to follow me or are you going to show me around."

"Were going to show you around chill gosh"

Max said this as if it was a joke.

“Ok here’s the gym and there are the locker rooms the class rooms are down there the first one is for science the 2nd is our room and the others are 6th and 8th grade”

Then the bell rang after what seemed like 2 minuets had actually been 15. She walked into her only separate class science with a teacher named Mrs. Mayberry she was In her sixties was plump and smelled like soap she simply wrote the lesson on the board and they were supposed to do it Christian had no problem but she could tell Natasha was puzzled and confused it made Christian laugh inside even though she could never laugh out loud. Time seemed to race after that and soon it was time for lunch. Christian was sitting at a table alone and Natasha was sitting in front of her but as soon as she saw costing and max sit down she moved.

“Hey max” Natasha said as sassy as ever “are you going to the dance on Friday?”

“No”

Max said quickly and emotionless Natasha’s face grew red and she looked like she was going to cry she got up and ran to the bathroom. Christian wanted to say at least she gets a taste of her own medicine but she couldn’t talk like that the last thing she wanted was to be like her.

Christian got up from lunch and walked up to her class room she had nothing better to do and then she notice that it was early release this made her very happy she picked up her backpack and left. At least 2 minuets into the walk home she saw max and costing coming up next to her.

"Hey you guys"

"Hi Christian you walk home well yes I guess so"

"Where's your house"

"Umm ok creepy question"

She said laughing as she pointed towards her house they said goodbye as they turned the other corner and Christian was then alone a few steps later she saw a black van with two men in it following her she started to run luckily they didn't follow. Christian walked through her front door as usual her dad wasn't home. She dropped her backpack and sat on the couch to watch TV she had finished all her homework so she was board and had nothing to do. 20 minuets later she walked over to the phone there was a message.

"Hey Christian it's me and Costin meet us at the park tomorrow morning at 6:00 ok bye"

That was odd Christian thought and continued to watch TV.

Two: taken by surprise

Thanks to Max and Costin Christian had to wake up very early that morning she got up brushed her teeth pulled her hair back in a pony tail and slipped on jeans and a T-shirt she jumped on her bike and made the 2 mile journey to the park when she got there she couldn't see costing or max where were they she then was grabbed and had a piece of cloth tied around her mouth and pulled into a van there she saw costing and max with the same piece of cloth tied around there mouth then they where given a shot and Christian fell into a deep sleep while sleeping she had the scariest dream of her life she could see her mom and costing and max all trapped somewhere and not able to get out but she couldn't do anything about it she kept trying to help but she couldn't . When she woke up from the terrifying dream she was in some sort of conference room with a few other kids including max and Costin. They all had glasses filled with sparkling water witch Christian thought was tacky considering they had no idea what was happening. Then a woman dressed as if she worked for a bank walked in hello everyone I’m Sarah I work for the ASI or the American security investigation. You all are going to be with us for a while so you might as well get comfortable each of you have a key in front of you this is the key to your room when you get there you will find a phone you may call your parents they don’t know where you are but they know why you’re here so you shouldn’t worry ill see all of you later until then please don’t create any problems your working with adults so you will be treated like adults.

Christian was still puzzled by everything that was going on she walked into her room that looked some what like a Hilton hotel room and called her dad her dad picked up and was very calm he told her not to worry and that he was close with the program and that she would get to see him soon. Christian was now confident that she was going to be fine and that she would be in good hands.

Three: Training for something great

There was a knock at Christian's room door she opened it was Sarah she told Christian it was time for her first training session this would consist of 4 courses fitness, aim, mental strength and weaponry Christian didn't know what was in store but she was looking forward to whatever it was. When she entered the training room she was surprised by how big it was it was about the size of a large gym there she was told to do 50 push ups she was capable and out of breath she finished even though it was a huge accomplishment for her to the trainers it seemed like nothing she was then told to do 50 sit ups this seemed like torture but she knew if she didn't obey there would be consequences she was then told to do at least 20 pull ups and that's where she just about reached her breaking point although finished she was out of breath and sore would she have to do this every day? An hour later after resting Christian was brought into a new room where there was a Glock hand gun waiting for her she was told to take 100 shots at the target she did this in stride getting it close to the middle 99% of the time what was with these instructors Christian thought to herself no matter how hard she tried all they would do is nod there heads every once in a while. 15 minuets later she was yet again brought into another room and given a piece of paper with 300 math problems she finished in 30 min and left feeling frustrated and sad how could an adult treat a child like this she thought why can they do this? After a long day of work she got into bed and slept restlessly. She had a dream there where 2 men fighting over a piece of paper with numbers all over it a man with a scar on his hand took the piece of paper and shot the other man. Christian woke up doused in a cold sweat what was that piece of paper and what did it mean.

Christian woke up that morning and took the other way to break fest there was a long gray hall way with art lining the walls mostly abstract you could tell the painting where meant to fill the void in the wall but not cause any emotion just before the door to the cafeteria she noticed a picture with the name Kayla Mantan on it this woman was obviously glorified according to all the awards on her chest the odd thing about this woman was that she looked almost identical to Christian she kept walking but couldn't forget the woman.

4: the strange man and a piece of paper

After finishing a disgusting breakfast of cornflakes and bananas she walked back to her room and switched on the news apparently there was breaking news a man age 31-34 murdered in abandoned hanger not identified if known please call 457-77777-90876 wow Christian thought that's weird and then a picture was shown it was the man in her dream she immediately told Sarah about the strange coincidence. Christian was then brought into a small room where the woman she saw in the picture was sitting hello Christian she said.

"I heard you have noticed your ability and by now you're wondering what is going on"

"Yes well I am wondering what's going on but I don't have a special ability"

“Yes you do Christian you see that’s the only reason we brought you here you see things in your dreams that are really happening at that very second”

“No I cant I’m not special I’m just an ordinary kid”

“Not anymore Christian that man that got murdered was working for us he had code 1000 a code to a virus that could kill millions if not billions of people the bottom line is we need you to help us get that code back or that man whatever his name might be will kill all of us here in America or maybe everyone all over the world”

“Well now that you say that I have to help how quick is he going to do this”?

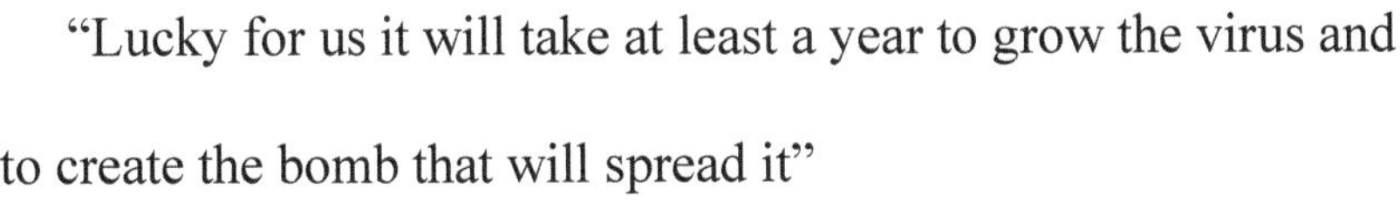

"Lucky for us it will take at least a year to grow the virus and to create the bomb that will spread it"

"Well then I guess we should get going"

"Not so fast unfortunately we have to start in one week right now all the information on the case is being sent to are lab"

"The rest of the week"

"Well ok what will I be doing"?

"You will be training even harder than before"

5: A Drill and more training

Everything was going as normal in the ASI until one morning at 3:00 a guard said they were under attack they were all put in bullet proof limos and taken to a huge tinted glass sky riser when they got inside turns out it was a hotel furnished with some of the fanciest furniture around. This was the first time Christian had seen max and costing for a while all of the other kids where gone besides them max said it was because they didn't pass the first training course which was actually a test. They stayed in that building for 2 days going over fire drills and earth quake drill in the end Christian found out all it was, was a drill. When they got back to ASI headquarters Christian was put through more extensive training including live battle being the scariest they were given fake guns to shoot with and would go into a live battle with each other max would usually kill costing first and then Christian would kill him making her the ultimate winner.

Christian went to bed the nigh after getting home from the drill and received a message from Kayla

"Hello Christian this is Kayla I would like to tell you the truth I am your mother I have missed you so much the years I have not been able to be with you your father and your sister once we solve this mission I will come home I didn't leave because I wanted to I left because I had to and your father knows that I just didn't want you to know because it would be to hard I'm sorry"

Christian was flabbergasted she didn't want to believe she could have been with her mom this whole time she now wanted to go home more than ever with her mom so they could be a family again they hadn't been a family in so long they could move back to Oregon and go back to there old friends and her old school but in her heart she knew it couldn't and wouldn't happen for a very long time she felt left down by her mother she knew she was her mother but when she found out she didn't want to run up and hug her she wanted to run back to her old friends and old house and never meet her mother ever again she felt as if she didn't have a mother at all even though on that very day she had found out where her mother had been all along and she said she loved her but how could Christian believe she cried all night long trying not to scream she forced herself to go to bed where she had the same dream as a while ago …….Her Mother, Costin, Max , Zoe and her Dad were all stuck but this time it seemed like every time she would open the door her mother would close it shut and then they all disappeared and she was the one who was stuck and her mom had the key and she was screaming for help but her mother acted as if she couldn't hear her and walked away and she was all alone in a dark room . Christian woke with a start someone had opened her door it was Max he said he had heard her screaming from down the hall and wondered what was going on all Christian said was she had a bad dream and started to cry silently. Christian got up the next morning to the sound of yelling it was time for training she went into another training room and went into a boxing ring it was more physical training then max came in a worried look in his eyes.

"Today children you will be fighting I know its boy against girl but I don't want either of you to back down you got it good…START!"

Max walked up expecting Christian to block and punched her in the face Christian didn't try to fight back she just stood there and then fainted. Everything seemed to be going so fast she heard Max scream help and then someone picked her up and he said so remorsefully.

“Please god tell me I didn’t hurt her”

Then everything went black she heard voices mostly max and her mother asking the doctor if I was going to be ok Max was there the whole time Christian was in a coma every once in a while he would feel her head or check her pulse. Christian began dreaming she was back at home in Oregon her mom was there but it wasn’t her mom it was someone else and Max was next to her he said come here Christian but she couldn’t walk he kept beckoning her to come but she couldn’t and she tried to tell them but she couldn’t. Then next day she woke up Max ran over hugged her and kissed her on the cheek. All he could say was…

“I’m so glad your back”

6: The deed is done

While Christian was asleep a video chat had come in to the ASI regarding code 1000 the man who had taken it had some how gotten Christians name and said he was going to kill her if she tried to find out any more information now that Christians life was endangered Max was worrying about Christian he liked her and didn't want her to be in danger so he came up with a plan for the ASI he could ask Christian to try and find out where the man with the scarred hands was and then they could go and kill him not saying it would solve the code 1000 mystery but Christian would be safe and that was all that mattered to him. Then next day max went to Christian and told her about his plan and knowing Christian she said no why would I do that you have got to be kidding me did you even think about what could happen to me he's already threatened me once why don't we go and get him a little more angry smart Max real smart, Christian you don't understand I don't want you to get hurt that's why I want to do this, well obviously I don’t want to do it so lets rethink this plan a little bit, you know what fine you can think that but outside of your little happy world some people actually care about you and love you and don’t want you to get hurt. Christian couldn’t stand this anymore between max her mom and this man who wanted to kill her how much worse could her life get. Christian now lost of her best friend went to costing for help whom she hadn’t seen for week s what had he been doing?

“Hey Costin”

“Hey Christian how’s it going I haven’t seen you in forever but I heard you and Max are fighting”

“Well if he could stop being stupid I wouldn’t be fighting with him”

“Christian cut him some slack he likes you a lot the last thing he wants to do is fight”

“Well maybe if he could just agree a little more and argue a little less”

“Listen Christian I don’t know why but you’re not the Christian I used to know so try and be a little more like her and maybe that will work”

“Well I do hope so bye costing I guess ill say sorry to max”

“Good for you I’ll se you later bye”

Although things weren’t going her way she went to max’s room where she found him lying on his bed.

"Hey max I'm sorry for being a jerk I like being best friends not enemies please forgive me I'm so sorry I haven't been myself this week and I don't like it when we fight"

"I don't like to fight either but Christian sometimes you have to think about what other people might think about the situation you're my friend and I care about you but sometimes you take that as some sort of offense"

"I agree sometimes I tend to not like it when people care a lot about me because it stops me from being who I want to be and I don't like being told what to do by someone else"

"Well I can see where fighting again so I accept your apology anyway I miss being your friend"

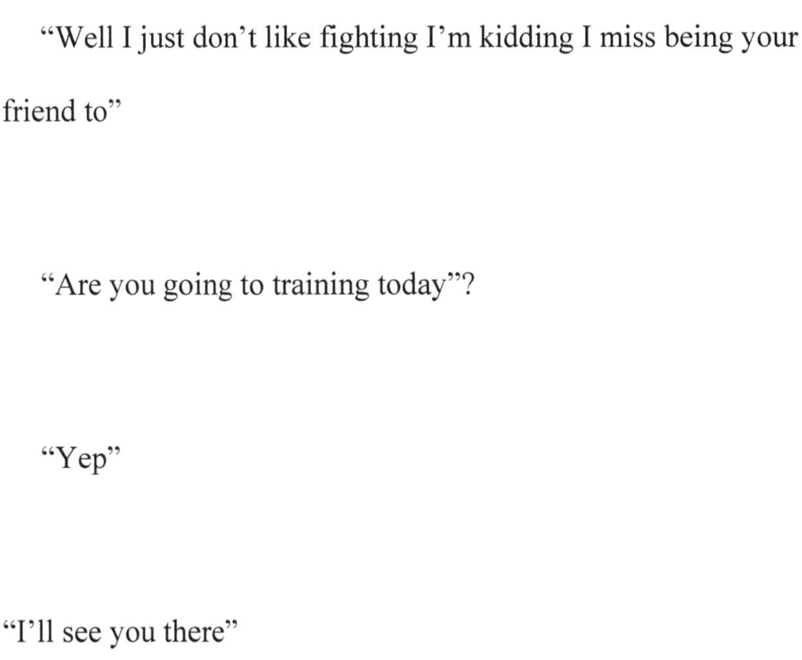

“Well I just don’t like fighting I’m kidding I miss being your friend to”

“Are you going to training today”?

“Yep”

“I’ll see you there”

Christian hadn't seen her mom since the phone call and she wondered where she was so she called her all she go was the answering machine and Christian left it at that things just were not right why where things suddenly beginning to be so weird Christian thought?

7:Missing or have they left

Christian woke up the next day to find her mother Costin and Max where all gone where were they Christian had to find out she remembered back to her dream many days ago when those exact same people were trapped somewhere and she told a sketch artist and according to her drawing they where in the basement of the burnt down senate office that had been replaced years ago this was a very serious moment when Christian was in complete and utter fear for the first time it was like being flipped upside down 200 to many times why her why her friends and family she had to help them if it was the last thing she did.

Christian took the first plane to Washington D.C that day and found the old us senate building she had already seen 5 guards and knew she wasn't getting in threw the main entrance but she did see a vent on the other side of the partially burnt building she some how managed to get through that vent and into the main building where a large man taped her he duct taped her mouth and rapped it around her legs and arms and tied her to a chair right in front of her she could see her mom, Costin and Max through a fiber glass window they were so close but so faraway she had to get out of there and fast.

Suddenly Christian remembered the training how to get out of this situation she brought her arms up and removed her mouth piece then removed her foot ties by stretching down and noticing her fingers were lose then she got her foot and applied trapped in and found the key she then unlocked her door and the door to lots of pressure to the wrist braces until the tape broke. She was free then by the bottom of the floor she noticed a vent she crawled to the door of the room she was Max, Costin, and her mom’s door. They where free her mom took out her concealed gun and shot to of the guards unfortunately the man with the scared hands was no there so they left with out code 1000.

8: sometimes things happen

Christian had just about met her limit when her mom came back to the ASI headquarters she couldn't stand to look at her it shouldn't have been so awkward but it was even worse then she had expected she tried to make small talk but it ended in 3 or 4 words why did everything get worse by the day the only good thing was that Max and Costin were ok that's all that mattered but she felt a twang of guilt each time she looked at her mom she looked so lonely or was that a look of sadness she couldn't tell although Christian couldn't look at Kayla like a mother she knew it was her mother and that she did love her even though sometimes it felt like she was the only person who was really Christians friend. The next day she talked to her mom they had had a long discussion and Christian ended the conversation with sometimes things happen because its true things happen that you may regret but you cant take them back. Things were now less weird with her mother and now her life was getting back on track it had been nearly 2 weeks since Christian had really gotten on track foe code 1000 and the case was getting stranger every day in 1 week the whole team will be going to France to see if the man with the scared hands is where they think he is unfortunately it classified information and not even Christian knew exactly where they where going. This worried Christian a lot how would she know what to do and what would happen if she didn't know what to do. Would her friends

Lives are in danger? The days coming up to the big trip were hectic and terribly difficult they where put through tedious training and difficult mental challenges would this situation be even worst then she had first thought. Now that Christian was on good terms with her mom you might say she had some one to tell every thing with out having to worry about what people would say but Christian felt uncomfortable with the fact that she hadn't seen her mom since she was 6 it made it hard to talk about things, her mom didn't know much about her life aside from the part that she was there for which surprisingly didn't seem that long and Christian knew that her mom felt no remorse for the pain she had caused did she really just think life had went on a usual because if she did she was dead wrong!

9: The night before Christmas

It was Christmas eve at the ASI and things were just about silent Christian was in her bed thinking about everything that had happened in the past year Christmas was not going to be the same with out her family Christian wasn't even sure if they celebrated Christmas here? Christian went to bed thinking about her dada and what he must be thinking right then on the night before Christians favorite holiday.

She woke up the next morning to the sound of the alarm clock and went to breakfast and there wasn't any thing that had to do with Christmas it was exactly the same this made Christians day even more dull than before she was not looking forward to staying here.

10: 3 months later the mission

Christian was in a helicopter flying to France it was 2:00 in the morning and she was desperately tired it was landing time and she could feel the plane decreasing in height when they landed Christian was quickly and rushed into a ware house where suddenly shots started going off she saw a strange man with a scar on his hand and quickly pulled the trigger and then fainted.

11: Back home

Christian woke up back in her new house with her mom by her side Christian wasn't sure what had happened but she was sure that she had gone back home her dad walked into the room with so hot coco and cookies.

Christian was Glad that it was final over and hoped there wouldn't be a next time but maybe there would.

The End

About the author

Madison Ebejer was born January 22nd, 2000 in Santa Barbra California she spent her first 3 years in Los Alamos California and then moved to Los Olivos California. she has now been there for 9 years. Madison lives with 1 dog, 2 cats, a Quarter horse and yes two parents named Cyndi and Dennis. Madison aspires to be a lawyer and maybe write in the meantime. Just in case you didn't know Madison is 12 and is in the 6th grade at Los Olivos Elementary. Madison has always thought how cool it would be to some kind of secret agent knowing this would never happen she wrote a book about the adventures of a girl who was shaped around the image of a tough but kind girl some even say that Christian might be dream Madison. Lots of inspiration came from Madison's parents and her teacher Mr. Rosenberg for helping with technical aspects and she would also like to thank Corner Hose Coffee for making a great "office" and having some of the best mochas around. Madison hopes that other young kids with dreams should write books because it’s a creative way to make them come true.

www.ingramcontent.com/pod-product-compliance
Ingram Content Group UK Ltd.
Pitfield, Milton Keynes, MK11 3LW, UK
UKHW041835200726
13854UKWH00003BA/1145